MW01017180

EYE TO EYE WITH HORSES

Thoroughbred Horses

Lynn M. Stone

Rourke
Publishing LLC
Vero Beach, Florida 32964

www.rourkepublishing.com

PHOTO CREDITS: All photos © Lynn M. Stone

Editor: Robert Stengard-Olliges

Cover and page design by Tara Raymo

Library of Congress Cataloging-in-Publication Data

Stone, Lynn M.
  Thoroughbred horses / Lynn Stone.
    p. cm. -- (Eye to eye with horses)
  ISBN 978-1-60044-583-5
  1. Thoroughbred horse--Juvenile literature. I. Title.
  SF293.T5S773 2008
  636.1'32--dc22
                                        2007019095

Printed in the USA

CG/CG

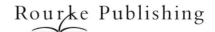

Rourke Publishing

www.rourkepublishing.com – rourke@rourkepublishing.com
Post Office Box 3328, Vero Beach, FL 32964

Table of Contents

Thoroughbred Horses

Thoroughbred horses are the world's best known racing horses. A Thoroughbred can run a mile (1.6 kilometers) at high speed faster than any other **breed** of horse. Most horse races cover about one mile.

Born to run, a California-born Thoroughbred foal keeps pace with its mother.

This is a very fine example of a Thoroughbred stallion.

Thoroughbred horses earned their fame on race tracks.

Thoroughbreds are not just for racing. But they have earned their fame and reputation on the track. Almost all the famous horses in North America have been Thoroughbreds. The film *Sea Biscuit* was about a famous Thoroughbred of the 1930's. A few other famous American Thoroughbreds were Citation, Man O' War, Secretariat, and, most recently, Barbaro.

THOROUGHBRED FACTS

Thoroughbreds are sometimes called "hot blooded." That means that Thoroughbreds are designed to be fast runners, not slow work horses. For the record, all horses' blood is the same temperature.

Thoroughbred fame usually comes from winning one or more of the three races in The Triple Crown of Thoroughbred Racing: The Kentucky Derby, Preakness Stakes, and Belmont Stakes. These three races are held once each year. A Thoroughbred that wins all three becomes a "Triple Crown winner." But it's a difficult task. The last horses to win the Triple Crown were Seattle Slew in 1977 and Affirmed in 1978.

*Seattle Slew, pictured long before his death in 2002,
relaxes in a Kentucky pasture.*

The History of Thoroughbred Horses

Thoroughbred racing is often called the "Sport of Kings." King Richard I may have organized England's first horse race. Henry VIII of England, king from 1509 - 1547, was a huge supporter of horse racing. James I set up the first race track at Newmarket. Charles II gave horse racing a boost in the 1660's.

The old English "running" horses were fairly fast. They were also a mix of breeds. Horse **breeders** of those days could not be sure what type of foals their **mares** and **stallions** would produce.

In the late 1600's, a Turkish stallion was imported to England. Soon after, two Arabian horse stallions were imported.

In the "Sport of Kings," racing Thoroughbreds get constant attention, like a sudsy wash.

These imported **purebred** horses mated with the English racing horses. The Arabians were used largely to improve the horses' racing endurance and **type**. With the addition of Arab blood, racing horse parents began to produce foals that were almost always of racing type.

Modern Thoroughbreds produce high quality foals of their "type."

English horse breeders added Arabian horse (shown here) bloodlines to produce the Thoroughbred.

Certain Arabian horses were mated with British racing horses until 1770. By then, British breeders had the new racing breed they wanted. The new breed was called the Thoroughbred.

The first Thoroughbred ancestor reached America in 1730. By 1873, American Thoroughbred owners had begun to keep careful records of their prized horses in a "studbook." Today the Jockey Club keeps the Thoroughbred record book.

The popularity of American horse racing grew as the country grew. Today billions of dollars are spent each year betting on Thoroughbred races. Billions more are spent buying and selling horses. And brand name manufacturers sponsor Thoroughbred races.

The Jockey Club keeps records of each Thoroughbred stallion (shown here) and mare and their offspring.

Being a Thoroughbred

Most Thoroughbreds in North America are raised on large farms. These are often known as "stables" or "stud farms."

Thoroughbred owners invest large sums of money in their horses and farms. The horses are handled with great care. They receive constant attention from workers at the farms. The horses are looked after by **farriers** and **equine veterinarians**. Other workers groom, wash, exercise, and train the horses.

Exercise and training prepare a young Thoroughbred for racing.

Thoroughbred farms have large exercise pastures. Many Thoroughbreds have daily workouts on race tracks.

A typical Thoroughbred is larger than its Arabian ancestors. It is about 15.2 **hands** (62 inches, 159 centimeters) high. Its coat is usually bay, chestnut, brown, black, or gray.

Thoroughbreds graze on a large Thoroughbred farm near Lexington, Kentucky.

Drying after being washed, Thoroughbreds walk on leads attached to an exercise wheel.

A Thoroughbred should have a long, graceful neck. Its head is trim with a largely straight face. It has fine, slender legs and powerful hind muscles for galloping. At full speed, a Thoroughbred can sprint up to 45 miles per hour (72 kilometers per hour).

Owning a Thoroughbred

A Thoroughbred can sell for more than one million dollars if it has great racing possibilities. But that doesn't mean that the average person can never own a Thoroughbred.

Not all Thoroughbreds make great race horses. Thoroughbred trainers know early in a horse's life if it should race.

This dappled gray Thoroughbred stallion was retired after an outstanding career as a racehorse.

Thoroughbreds that aren't likely to be racehorses are used for other purposes. They may be used for recreational riding or hunting. They are also used as polo horses and in jumping events.

Thoroughbreds can be good pleasure riding horses.

Glossary

breed (BREED) – a group of domestic animals within a group (such as Thoroughbred horses) having the same basic characteristics

breeder (bree DUR) – one who raises animals, such as horses, and lets them reproduce

equine veterinarian (ee KWINE vet ur uh NER ee uhn) – a horse doctor

farrier (FAIR ee uhr) – one who takes care of a horse's shoes and hooves

hand (HAND) – a 4-inch (10-centimeter) unit to measure the height to a horse's shoulder

mare (MARE) – an adult female horse

purebred (pur BREAD) – a domestic animal of a single breed, such as a purebred Thoroughbred

stallion (STAL yuhn) – an adult male horse that can father foals

type (TIPE) – one of a group with similar shape or form

Index

Further Reading

Dell, Pamela. *Thoroughbreds*. Child's World, 2007.
Diedrich, John. *The Thoroughbred Horse*. Capstone, 2005.

Website to Visit

www.kyhorsepark.com/imh/bw/tbred.html
www.ansi.okstate.edu/breeds/horses/thououghbred/indexhtm

About the Author

Lynn M. Stone is the author of more than 400 children's books. He is a talented natural history photographer as well. Lynn, a former teacher, travels worldwide to photograph wildlife in its natural habitat.